The Deliberate Collection

by

Natasja Rose

Table of Contents

The Squirrel's Debt

Another prompt from my writer's meet-up. "You swerve to avoid a squirrel. Unknown to you, the squirrel pledges a life debt. In your darkest hour, the squirrel arrives" captioning a picture of a squirrel in armour and holding a shield.

The street lights were out, the road dark and winding. That it was overcast and nearing midnight did not help the poor visibility. Neither did the car behind me, displeased at my slow, cautious pace, and not shy about showing it.

The other car's horn blared again, and something fell out of a tree just up ahead. I swerved to avoid hitting it, and nearly ran off the road. Why did I always run into the jerks when I was least in the mood for it?

Getting myself back on track, I let the asshole in the other car go around me, and slowly continued my drive, willing my racing heartbeat to calm down. Trying to remember the road rules in a foreign country was hard enough, I didn't need any more distractions.

The rest of the drive was uneventful, but I couldn't help feeling like something significant, something wonderful and life-changing, had happened.

Or not. I was hideously over-tired. It was probably just my imagination.

*   *   *

A year later, I wished that everything going on was just my imagination. The person in the car behind me, on that dark night, had been a modern-day necromancer.

Yeah, I was surprised, too. Turns out the D&D nerds were actually onto something, and a lot of game nights had an actual Necromancer, Cleric or occasional Orc show up, under the guise of a really dedicated player who came in costume that night.

Worse yet, said necromancer had decided that making him late for one such game qualified me to be his arch-nemesis. Talk about unreasonable drama-kings. Anyway, it took him a while to find my address... until last week, in fact, but since then it had been nothing but trouble.

Rotting animal corpses on my doorstep or in the driveway, reanimated bird skeletons tapping on my window just as I'm about to fall asleep and waking me up, tiny vole corpses in the vegetable garden...

Actually, I wasn't as upset as the Necromancer probably hoped about the last one. Apparently, dead bodies were really good for the plants. I wasn't about to let him know that, though.

As long as this was as bad as it got, I could survive until he got bored or found someone else to be his eternal enemy. I hoped so, anyway.

*　　*　　*

I take it back! I take it all back!

I had never been a fan of rats, even pet ones. I really wasn't a fan of hundreds of shambling, freshly-killed rats and mice flooding my lawn, and, from a glance out of the kitchen window, the back yard, too.

I dashed around the house, making sure every possible opening was shut, bolted or blocked. I tried to regulate my breathing, forcing away a panic attack. Being curled up on the floor, shaking and terrified, would only make the situation worse.

I wouldn't give that bloody Necromancer the satisfaction.

Outside the window, a flash of silver caught my eye.

It was a tiny squirrel, in an equally tiny suit of armor, clutching a miniture sword and shield. That wasn't unusual - some of the more artistic gamers were always subjecting their pets to costuming of some kind, and there were no shortage of memes of squirrels and cats in armor. Maybe the cats had all hidden before they could be dressed up this time.

What was unusual was when the squirrel streaked across the lawn and took up guard outside my front door, just as the first of the rats reached it.

A flash of steel, and the first of the rats fell back. A mouse jumped far further than any mouse should be able to, and bounced off a raised shield. Two more charged at once, and fell to a single swing.

The squirrel's sword must have been blessed or something - and isn't that something I never imagined myself saying unironically - because whatever rodent it touched fell to the ground and did not move again. After a few moments, the no-longer-animated corpses vanished in a shimmer of air.

My life was officially too weird for words.

*　　*　　*

Finally, the last of the rats and mice were gone, and I cautiously opened the door. The squirrel turned to face me, sword in what looked suspiciously like parade rest, and a keen intelligence in his eyes.

Well, it's not like my life could get any more absurd. "Er, are you a human under enchantment?"

My tiny saviour looked almost offended, and shook its head vigorously. That was a relief; I was in no mood to navigate the complexities of explaining that saving my life did not give him the right to my hand in marriage.

A scratching sound made me look down again, and I saw the squirrel using the point of its sword to draw something in the dust on my doorstep. A tree, and a squirrel in front of a car. It jogged my memory, "You're the squirrel who I nearly ran off the road to avoid hitting?"

The squirrel nodded, pleased, and continued drawing. A gravestone crossed out, and a money sign. A life debt? A clock and a patch that was just scratched out, revealing the dark stone underneath. Darkest hour? The plague of rats certainly counted.

A circle with a cross coming out, the symbol of femininity, and a wand. It seemed surreal, but what about any of this qualifed as normal? "I saved your life, so you owe me a debt, discharged now in my darkest hour. You are magical, though, and you're a girl squirrel."

Another nod, and I felt an odd pang of sadness. I knelt down, as close to the squirrel's level as I could get, and held out my hand. "Does this mean that you have to leave now?"

A chittering sound and a shake of her head. She hopped onto my hand, the armour vanishing, and curled up, butting her head against the pulse on my wrist. I smiled... I had always wanted a pet, and I had the perfect name, from the first warrior women I had read about. "Well, then... welcome home, Trebond."

Full Of Grace

Written for a Christmas Challenge, because Mary really doesn't get enough attention. Perhaps one day I'll write one for Joseph, too. Heavily inspired by The Nativity Story.

Through all of my faith, there is one thing that I have always questioned: Why did God choose me? Why did God think me worthy to bear His son, when I could not even promise him a good life? Nazareth was a tiny, impoverished village, and my family was not even among the prosperous, barely managing to pay taxes year to year.

I had performed no great deeds or worthy acts, nor had the Lord seen fit to bless me for my husband's virtue, as he had my cousin Elizabeth. Sometimes I wonder if our sons will even meet, if they will be a rock for each other as Elizabeth and I were.

Why would the Lord choose me, newly married to a good and honest man, but still with my parents and a virgin? God would protect me from losing my child or miscarrying, but how to stop my own village stoning me as an adulteress? How was I to care for my son if I was divorced by my husband and cast out by my family, as was often the case for women who bore a child out of wedlock.

Joseph cared for me, I knew, and had cared long before he asked me to wife. Even knowing that I did not yet love him, he cared for and protected me still.

Knowing this, could I ask him to raise a son not his own? The son of God, yes, a divine blessing rather than the proof of betrayal, but not *his*.

*   *   *

I could have claimed that I was attacked by Roman soldiers, whose thirst for blood was matched only by their thirst for gold and flesh. No-one would have faulted me for a pregnancy in that case, but if they did not encourage me to get rid of it, the lie would have followed my child all of his life. It would taint him in the eyes of those he meant to save, just as many villagers did not look at Alia the same way, after the soldiers who came with the tax collectors brought her back.

My Jesus would be the son of God, the saviour of our people. His life would not be easy, and I would not make it harder with a lie to ease my own path. I trusted God to guide and protect me, and spoke only the truth.

Joseph was upset when I returned from Elizabeth's home visibly pregnant, and I could not blame him, but proved himself an even better man than I had already known. To protect me from a trial, he would risk his good name, knowing that people would talk. For the first time, I felt a flicker of love, not merely gratitude for his selfless acts.

What would happen after I gave birth no-one had decided. Joseph did not claim responsibility for my condition, but neither would he make any accusation, and as my husband, he was the only one with the right to demand a trial.

When he sought me out days later, I knew that there had been more to his dream than merely the appearance of an angel, but I did not press. If he did not tell me, it was doubtless for a good reason. We talked more, coming to know each other and finding strength together in the face of the village's silent disdain.

*   *   *

As my time grew closer, I started to dream of a star, guiding me to a different place. When the census was announced, and Joseph said that he could not register in Nazareth, it made sense: the star would guide us to the place where my child would be born.

Even if I had not dreamed of it, there was only one reply I could give my parents, "I am going with my husband."

If what I felt for Joseph was love, I could not say, but my place was at his side, and I knew that he would keep me safe.

The journey was long, and dangerous, and somehow I knew that it would be many years before I saw Nazareth or my family again, but I did not fear. When at last we came to Bethlehem, when I went into labour even as we passed the city gates, I trusted in God and in Joseph, and was not afraid.

A stable was not the ideal place to give birth, but it was the only room there was, when other doors were closed to us. Surrounded by animals rather than midwives, resting on a rough blanket with only a trough of straw to serve as a cradle and Joseph's *Yarmulke* to serve as a pillow, I brought my son into the world.

We had only a few minutes to ourselves, Joseph, Jesus and I, but in those moments I was happier than I thought possible. The shepherds came, warned by the angel, bringing what food and blankets they could. The Wise Men followed, bringing kingly gifts and lofty declarations.

It took longer than perhaps it should have before Joseph managed to send them away, so that Jesus and I could rest, only to be woken again when the angel sent a warning, telling us to flee to Egypt.

*   *   *

I will not presume to know His will, but perhaps the very reasons I felt unworthy were the reasons I was honoured. For all that the rich have, a sense of charity is rarely among it. The powerful and influential seek first their own advancement, rarely sparing thought for those who are powerless.

For God's son, my son, to be a leader of all men, he must *know* all men, not merely those who have power. To be a helper of men, he must witness what help they need, and know how to talk to them.

From a refugee seeking shelter, seen as the lowest of the low, Jesus would see the evils of the world, and learn to look past it to the good beneath.

Well, whatever the future holds, Jesus is my son, and Joseph the best of husbands. They are my family, and whatever else we may be, I will love and cherish them.

Let Us Write

Written during NaNoWriMo 2018, when there was a trend toward parody Disney songs themed around writing. To the tune of 'Let It Go'. Perhaps this year I'll see if we can do a music video...

There's the NaNo lock-in happening tonight

Lots of writers to be seen

We're shut in group isolation,

I'll be the NaNoWriMo Queen

The words are swirling all around inside my brain

Got to get them out, or I'll go insane.

No writer's block, no distractions,

Stop checking status reactions

My word count's up upon the screen

I'm gonna scream....

Let us write, let us write,

More word-sprints are in store

Let us write, let us write,

Who needs sleep after all?

The coffee's poured, I have my snacks

Let the timer start…

Time for #writerhacks

It's funny how excess coffee

Made me write this out of spite

Now I'm six thousand words in,

And there's no end in sight!

Five minutes left before we're through

I've got this, I really do!

No right, no wrong, no rules for me.

Writing spree!

Let us write, let us write

We are one with the word and plot

Let us write, let us write,

We're all here in one spot.

It's NaNo month, and so we write

Let us word-sprint on….

My plot line flurries from my mind onto the
page

My characters can't decide if they're Magician
or Mage

And one question breaks in through the caffeine
haze

My novel's just begun, how did my word count
reach this stage?

Let us write, let us write

Tumblr prompts and Q and A,

Let us write, let us write

Short stories carry the day

The clock ticks down and the drinks run low

Let us all write on

It's Lock-in Night and we're on the go.

Going on a Tangent

For the writing prompt: "Pack your bags, we're going on a tangent".

Inspired by a very stressful work meeting where my manager called five minutes before the meeting started, asking me to run it. I was in a truly vile mood at my writer's circle that night, and wrote this as an alternative to calling HR and quitting out of pure frustration at my useless co-workers.

"Pack your bags, we're going on a tangent."

It was a familiar phrase between my co-worker and I, developed over several months of office staff who couldn't stay on topic during a meeting if you offered them a $5 per hour raise.

I leaned back in the uncomfortable chair, resigned to my fate. It was a lot harder to take minutes when everyone was talking over each other and constantly veering away from the subject we were supposed to be discussing. Of course, perhaps I should count my blessings while I had them; the next topic was the (over)use of mobile phones in the workplace, and I already knew how that was going to go.

I switched windows, and under the guise of taking notes, turned the screen just enough for my co-worker to see the typed message. "I told you we were never going to get out of here on time."

A slight narrowing of the eyes and downward turn of their lips was the only answer they could give. I braced myself for impact, forcing the meeting back on track. "Next item: I've had customers complaining that staff are using their personal phones too much. If you need to check your messages or reply to a text or missed call, wait until you're on break or grabbing a drink. Don't do it in front of the customers; it's a bad look and we *just talked about* professionalism in the workplace."

There was a brief pause, and I chose to believe that they were actually considering the statement, rather than reeling in disbelief at the near-sacrilege of my words. As before, it was a vain hope. One, probably the most guilty of the staff, spoke up.

I held no hope that she would be asking for clarification, but I was still depressed to be proven right. "But it's not like we're leaving them dangling in the hoist while we run off to make a call. What if it's important?"

 THAT was her best case scenario? Did she want an award for not physically endangering a customer in favour of texting? Still, she did have a very minuscule point. It wouldn't be the first time Rostering called one of us to fill a shift on short notice. "If it's rostering, ask them if you can step outside and call back. That isn't a problem."

I suppose I should be grateful that the second-biggest culprit had actually managed to let someone else finish talking. "But what if it's family? My daughter is catching public transport to school for the first time and I need to check that she is awake, that she has caught the correct bus and that she gets to school!"

I bit back the uncharitable reply that they should have taken a day off to escort their child, or used a few hours on the weekend to travel-train their kids, and that all they were doing was making their daughter dependent. Or even, god forbid, get their work-from-home husband to pick up the slack. That would only result in me being yelled at, I knew from extensive prior experience, and their speaking voice was already argument-volume as it was.

"Then set your phone to vibrate and get her to call you *if* she encounters a problem and needs advice."

Yet another co-worker interjected. "Oh, my mother worries so much, too. If I don't answer the phone when she calls, she'll get so upset."

That co-worker's mother needed to back off and realise that they weren't twelve anymore, or the co-worker needed to find a job that they could do from home. Either one, I didn't really care, as long as it didn't create more paperwork for me.

Was it really that hard to sit a parent down and promise to call them before and after their shift, but that they wouldn't be able to answer calls while on the clock? I'd managed that conversation at fifteen, when I sometimes stayed behind to finish cleaning at the end of a shift at a fast food joint.

I gave up on getting anything else done as the rest of the staff promptly started defending their use of mobile phones during shift, completely missing the original point. I tilted my head back, closed my eyes for a moment and shifted my arm just enough to nudge the co-worker who was rapidly escalating from 'favourite' to 'the only one I can stand on a regular basis'. Le sigh. "Pack your bags, we're going on a tangent. We might actually need to take holiday leave."

My co-worker scoffed. "If it gets us away from this bunch, I'm cool with that."

The Murder Mystery

From a writing prompt as a 'get better soon' gift to my now-girlfriend, then-friend. It eventually became a longer novelette, but this was the original version.

Ramona really, really hated her family's insistence on setting her up on blind dates. She found relationships so much easier when she was writing them, and could actually make sense of both party's actions and motivations. Also, with her characters, she didn't have to deal with complaints that she made no sense and was a 'creepy weirdo'.

This time, Ramona's sister had bribed her with the promised loan of her kitchen next time Ramona needed to cook in bulk, and the assurance that this dating site found matches based on search history and common interests.

That, at least, made her morbidly curious about the person she would be meeting. At worst, they could at least talk about interesting topics until Ramona's dating obligations were fulfilled.

Ramona was a writer; specifically a crime and thriller writer. 'Interesting' was the nicest possible way to describe her search history. 'Creepy' and 'potentially criminal' were far more common terms. That the dating site had actually found someone to match her up with was kind of impressive.

*   *   *

Josh felt kind of guilty going on a blind date, with a person who might turn out to be genuinely nice. He hadn't had much luck with blind dates in the past, since most of them found him off-putting or boring, and they never seemed to have anything in common.

He never killed them, since they never treated him badly enough to deserve it, but it got depressing after a while. He hoped that a dating site that matched people based on search history and common interests might turn up someone who would at least be able to carry on an interesting conversation.

Josh was a serial killer, targeting people who deserved it; Mafia Bosses, CEOs who exploited their workers and used questionable business practices, politicians who allowed themselves to be bought by vested interests... People the world was honestly better off without. He was doing a public service, really, albeit one that would probably get him arrested if anyone found out. Then again, sit-ins in a segregated bar used to be grounds for arrest and imprisonment, too, so clearly there was a sliding scale for illegality.

Well, perhaps the date would go well, and perhaps it wouldn't. Perhaps he would even find out about the shitty ex- who treated them horribly enough to warrant being Josh's next victim.

*   *   *

The dating site also set up a convenient meeting place for the date, in this case a quiet coffee house in the BoHo part of town. Ramona got there early, found the table booked in their name - apparently her date was a guy called Josh - and pulled out her notebook. She had fifteen minutes, possibly even more if her date shared the previous one's tardiness, so she might as well get some writing done.

Besides, sometimes it scored her a free drink, if the owner believed in supporting independent artists.

Lost in her work, she jumped a little, pen skittering across the page, when a voice like hot chocolate came from beside her, "Sorry to interrupt, are you Ramona?"

She looked up, and then up some more. The man who interrupted her was tall, with lean but defined arm muscles, mostly revealed by the short-sleeved button-down he wore. His jeans weren't so tight to be able to tell if his legs matched, but Ramona was willing to make an educated guess. Well, he would make a nice character description for her next male lead, even if he turned out to be an internet troll living in his mother's basement. "Yes, hi. You're Josh?"

His smile was as nice to look at as the rest of him. "Yes, hi. Sorry, I didn't think I was running late."

Ramona shook her head, "Oh, no, I was early. There turned out to be less traffic than I thought, so I had time to kill."

Josh sat down across from her, and earned instant points by not trying to play footsie. "What are you working on, if you don't mind me asking?"

Well, at least they could get the awkward out of the way early. "I'm a crime fiction writer. This will hopefully become the outline for my next book."

There was a gleam of interest in his eye, which earned him even more points, upgrading Josh to 'text and thank for a nice date' status. "What's it about?"

*   *   *

Josh wasn't sure what falling in love was supposed to feel like, but he was pretty sure that it felt like this.

Ramona's detailed descriptions of the detective who kept barely missing the killer, the race against time, the anticipation of the victims who knew that they were going to be next... he took back every bad thing he had ever said about dating sites. This one had matched him up with the most perfect woman on the face of the planet. A first date was probably too soon to start planning a life together, wasn't it? Maybe an exception could be made?

Ramona paused for breath, and he took the opportunity to contribute, so she would know that he was actually listening, rather than faking it. He didn't want to mess this up. "What's the villain's motivation? Like, subconscious trauma? Skewed morality but wants to make the world better? Or just in it for the adrenaline rush."

The way her face lit up took Josh's breath away, and she gestured to her notebook. "I don't mean to be rude, but do you mind if I write this down?"

She could ask him to sit in an abandoned car for hours, and he would probably agree at this point. "Oh, go ahead."

Josh waited a few minutes, before he dared to interrupt. "Out of curiosity, how would you kill someone and make it look accidental?"

Ramona barely looked up, her distracted tone comparable to the most beautiful music he had ever heard. "Air shot between the toes. Makes it look like a heart attack."

Josh swallowed hard, pushing down a surge of arousal. Oh, yes, he was in love.

*   *   *

Ramona was pleasantly surprised by how well the date was going.

Josh hadn't once mocked her, and seemed genuinely interested in everything she had to say. He hadn't even complained or become offended when she pulled out her notebook to start scribbling, but casually pulled a book out of his backpack, sipping coffee while he waited for her to finish. Looking at the title, Ramona recognised the book as one with an author who actually did their research. "Hey, do you know how long it would take someone to die from a stab to the gut?"

Immediately, she winced, hoping that she hadn't just committed some weird and unintentional faux pas. He didn't get up and run out of the cafe, which was something, but his eyes did darken slightly. Ramona didn't think it was with anger, though, and he tilted his head to the side, thinking. "Two minutes to half an hour, it depends on a variety of factors."

Was a first date too early to start thinking about wedding rings? Ramona thought that the answer was probably 'Yes - way too fast.'

A pity, that; a gold and platinum ring, with an inlaid ruby or two, would look amazing on him.

*   *   *

Josh worked as a Butcher's assistant, but he always made sure to shower and change before he came home.

They had both received some very askance looks from family members after moving in together after only a few months, but they didn't care. Ramona didn't freak out when there was the occasional bloodstain to be washed out of his clothing, and he thought it was adorable when she bought her notebook to the table, writing between bites.

This one was new, Ramona having just finished filling up her old one. She looked up from her writing as Josh finished his coffee. "Babe, I'm not sure if this murder scene I'm writing is realistic enough. Can you look it over and tell me?"

Josh could do one better than that; he could actually test it out. "Mind if I take it to work with me and read it over? I'll tell you when I get home tonight."

Ramona smiled happily at him. "Sure. I should probably get my old notebook transcribed onto my computer, anyway."

Josh kissed her on the cheek on his way out the door. "I might be a bit late coming home, one of the other staff wasn't feeling well yesterday, and I might need to cover. I'll be home in time for dinner, promise."

Ramona nodded and waved goodbye, already searching for her charger. She'd probably be spending the day at her favourite cafe, staffed with people who didn't care how long she took up a table, so long as she kept buying drinks and gave the employees something to during the lull period. Josh had already decided that he would probably never need to visit any of them.

On the other hand, there was a customer who had taken to making one of the trainees' life difficult; complaining about everything and threatening to call the immigration police or local law enforcement. Josh seriously doubted that anyone would actually miss him.

*   *   *

He didn't manage to completely wash away the smell of blood before he got home - he didn't want to be late, not after promising Ramona that he would be on time for dinner. She didn't seem to mind as he handed back her new notebook. "It works perfectly, babe, you're doing an amazing job."

Ramona beamed, putting the finishing touches on the pasta dish she was making. He knew for a fact that she threw it together in half an hour, but that wasn't important. "Oh, a co-worker read it over my shoulder and asked if you were re-writing Sweeny Todd or something. I think that's the only near-horror thing he's ever looked at, honestly."

Ramona huffed. "Not hardly, Sweeny was an idiot, and Mrs. Lovett's pies shouldn't have sold half so well. Adult meat is mostly muscle; cooking it slowly in a pie would make it far too tough and gamey. They would have done better to go for foundling babies. Steady supply, their absence would be barely noticed, and fatty meats are far more tender, anyway."

Josh wrapped his arms around her. "Have I mentioned lately how much I love you?"

The Game

Loosely inspired by the 2017 Jumanji movie, this was a thought that became a few lines that became a writing exercise. Comparative Mythology and magical things that teach deserving mortals valuable lessons have always been my weakness.

The Game did not know how it came to be, or why.

Some, if they thought about it at all rather than trying to suppress the memory, believed The Game a trap from the Fair Folk, trouble in a harmless guise, for the cruel amusement of the Lords and Ladies. Others suggested a Trickster's gift, a blessing and a second chance disguised in trauma and terror. Yet more wondered if it might not be an unlawful djinn, gone mad from imprisonment and cursing itself into a new form, to grant a wish that the even the finder was unaware of, lingering malice driving it to do so in as cruel a way as possible.

The players themselves rarely had time for such philosophical questions, more concerned with survival, and then with doing their very best to hide or destroy the game. The Game laughed to itself when they did, amused at their petty attempts. As if one with the power to bend reality could be so easily thwarted. But it was pleasing that they retained enough hope to think it possible, so The Game allowed them their illusions.

If The Game cared to dwell on its origins, in the long years between players, it thought that it was probably none of the things that people supposed, yet all of the theories had an element of truth.

It had a consciousness, of sorts, an awareness unbound by empathy or morality, and a purpose, though the fine details varied between players. Its power, its very existence, was bound to that purpose.

The Game's first player had been a young girl, scared and uncertain, unwilling to face the duty that came with her privilege. The Game gave her the adventure she didn't know she wanted, the wisdom to realise that her choices had consequences, and the skills she needed to achieve her potential.

She thanked The Game by having it trampled in a stampede, much like the ones she had experienced. The Game, then only a set of dice and a list of actions, laughed to itself as the clay shattered and parchment tore. It would be back.

*   *   *

The Game had its favourites, over the years.

Jacob Sherman, an arrogant bully whose fellow players, playing a game found while raiding a place sacred to the natives they saw as little different to the animals they hunted, finished the game without rolling the 5 or 8 needed to free him. Jacob responded by allowing his bitter cruelty to overtake him, hunting the other residents of the Jungle in an attempt to slake his fury. The Game was disappointed at Jacob's failure to accept the offer to improve himself, and never allowed him to succeed in his hunts.

*   *   *

Allistair Parks, an intelligent but fearful boy who had the potential to thrive to greatness, but not without some external help. His parents protected him too much to force him to face his problems, and none of them had yet managed to bridge the communication gap. Allan would have to be the one to make the first move, and to do that, he needed to learn to rely on himself.

The Game lured him to discovery with the sound of drums, and Allan followed with a will. Allan thrived in the crucible that was the Jungle, and the game protected him just enough to ensure that he survived to return home.

*   *   *

Adrien Van Reek was a special favourite, who loved The Game because it was a game, but needed to learn to live outside of games every so often. The Game guided him to Allistair's old home, gave him a place of safety and helped him avoid the traps until he knew where they were. Adrien would survive, and learn what his fellow players would need when they arrived. He awoke to the sound of drums, and followed them to his destiny.

The Game had been a board game for centuries before Adrien gave it the opportunity to transform into something new. The Game relished the opportunity to expand into something new, something so much more than it had been. It rejoiced, and slowed time in the Jungle, so that Adrien would not need to linger too long between his arrival and return.

*   *   *

The other four were a delight. Two of each, desperately trying to ignore the problems plaguing them, needing The Game's help more than they would ever know. They would be perfect companions for Adrien.

The two girls who needed to find true, supportive friendships, polar opposites who were not so different as they thought. One who needed to live life, rather than endure it while chasing some undefined goal. One who needed to stop relying on external validation and appearances, and own her decisions.

Two boys who needed to mend the gulf between them, who had so much buried anger and hurt, wounds that needed to be lanced in order to heal, that they would never confront on their own. One hurt by abandonment, so desperate to regain a lost friendship that he did not realise how much he was hurting himself in an unhealthy parody of that relationship, who needed to stand up for himself and his wants, to realise that being himself was enough. He and the first girl would help each other far longer than simply their time in the Jungle, if they gained the courage. The Game thought them adorable, as much as it could feel anything.

The last was a walking contradiction. He seemed to have life the best of all of them, yet was the one most in need of The Game's intervention. He had been in a position of social power and respect, yet internally was filled with so much fear and insecurity that it made him cruel to those who had once been friends. The game forced him to the bottom of the power structure, forced him to realise that even in the position he feared the most - *weak, helpless, a burden* - he still had value, as did the ones he scorned.

*   *   *

The Game was pleased when the five players learned their lessons as well as they did, succeeding in all the challenges that The Game threw their way.

They blossomed in the fires of Adversity, forged themselves in the crucible of the Jungle, and emerged stronger and better for it.

The Game laughed when they destroyed it, with as much determination and thoroughness as the noble daughter, the first of The Game's players, had. The outside world was changing swiftly, and already the game needed a new form than the one Adrien Van Reek had given it.

As ever, The Game would return, when there was one nearby who needed the lessons it taught, who would hear the drums and follow them to what they would become.

How The Dragon Was Slain

Written for a competition, based around a dragon-themed event. After helping run the Children's Quest, I needed a break, so I wrote this around the Quest.

Pray heed, honoured guests, and hear now the tale of the dragon of the Acorn Lands.

Once, there was a dragon, who left the land of his birth and became terribly lost. After long weeks and months of travel, he found himself in a land of oak trees and purple acorns, ruled over by a mighty king.

The people of the land, finding themselves much troubled by the dragon, organised a tourney, reasoning that only the mightiest of champions could slay the beast. Warriors came from far and wide, from the land of the Rowan and the Griffon and of the Acorn itself, and even from the far western borders.

 Some were of great renown, having practiced their craft for many years. Some were untested, seeking glory on the field. All were determined to triumph over the others and win the title of Champion.

*   *   *

While the tourney took place, the children of the realm gathered together. Now, as all parents know, leaving small children unsupervised in a situation where they might happen upon a most excellent idea, will always lead to trouble. The children reasoned that many swords were more effective than one… even if that one was more experienced, and an adult. Banding together, they travelled in groups, for everyone knows that Quests are more fun with friends.

*   *   *

Now it came to pass that in this land also dwelled a noble lady of great courage and compassion, who in her youth had found an abandoned nest, and raised the eggs therein to three smaller dragons of her own.

 As is the way of children, these three dragons had now grown and moved away. If the Questing Children would visit the three dragons, and bring back news of them, the lady would give them something to help them in their quest.

The children visited each dragon in turn, and each group was set a task, no two side-quests the same. This was, the dragons claimed, so that the children could carry news back to their Mother that they were not just sitting on their hordes all day.

Thus assured, the Lady gave each child some shiny coins, with which to distract the great beast who plagued their lands. As all educated people know, there is nothing the Great Dragons crave so much as bright gold.

*   *   *

The coins were indeed shiny, but they were not true coins, being filled with a tasty treat.

Now, on a quest, there are no rules about bedtime, or in what order dinner and dessert are eaten, or in what quantities. Some of the children, paying less heed to the commands of their wise elders, had eaten the coins by the time they faced the dragon, and were forced to flee before their wrath.

But finally, there came one group who were good children, who obeyed their parents' rules, and had not eaten their coins.

These coins they scattered widely over the ground before the Dragon's cave, and waited in ambush, with blade and arrow at the ready.

 The dragon emerged, for the lure of shiny things outweighed any danger that might lurk nearby. The great beast gathered the coins one by one, and when his hands were full and he moved slowly, so as to not drop the coins and have to gather them a second time, they attacked. The children fell upon him with sword and shield and cries of triumph.

So great was their enthusiasm, so boundless their energy, that the dragon was made fearful. He fled before their fury, and vowed to return nevermore to the Acorn Lands.

*   *   *

The children returned to the village hall, where the tourney was just concluding, no less than the Mighty King himself having claimed Victory over all comers.

The king was much dismayed that the dragon was no longer available for him to fight, and even moreso that both of his children, a son not yet seven and a daughter younger yet, had been instrumental in its defeat.

But the cooks of the Acorn Lands were held in great renown, and with very good reason. There was a feast to celebrate, so all in the tale ended the day happily, and with many tasty leftovers.

Surviving a Zombie Apocalypse

You know all of those Facebook and Tumblr posts about how to survive a theoretical Zombie Apocalypse (vs the Survivalist ideas of 'stock up on guns and shoot anything that moves)? This was my response to reading a few too many of those.

No-one knew how the plague that turned the world into a dystopian zombie nightmare began.

Some said it was a communicable disease, transmittable through bodily fluids. Some said it was like rabies, passed on through a bite. Others claimed that it struck at random, and a few even that it was divine punishment.

In the end, how it began didn't matter; the only concern was survival.

*   *   *

At first, all mention of a Zombie Apocalypse was met with a combination of giggles, eye-rolls and muttering about out-of-control hoaxes.

When an emergency broadcast went out went out in the middle of a Games Night, they took it a bit more seriously. Mary put down her cards - it had been a shit hand, anyway - and headed for the pantry. "Who do we know who lives outside the city and is unaffected?"

Trixie joined her in stuffing cans and long-life food into bags, calling over her shoulder to her husband. "Grab the toolkit and any seed packets we have, love, then call around."

Kel headed out to the garage, taking Tim with him. "We'll get the camping stuff, too."

Bella looked up from her phone. "Steve and Ali are both in the clear, and as long as we're willing to test to prove ourselves clean, issuing an open invitation. It's a two-hour drive, but we can make it."

Mary nodded, reaching for a replica sword that, while not top quality, would still work, and handed Bella a bow and quiver. "Let's go unload anything useless from the cars. We'll want to get a move on."

Trixie headed for the bedrooms where her children slept. "Let Kel know that we don't need the pram, and to hitch up the trailer. Keep whatever sewing and weaving supplies you have living in there, too. We'll need those soon enough."

Bella grinned. "We just got a delivery of fabric. Plenty of wool and linen."

Mary high-fived her. "And they said that my Living History interests would never come in useful."

Tim scoffed, walking back in with an armful of propane cylinders. "Yeah, like the idiots whose grand plan is to shoot everything that moves and rely on loot drops would last a week without us."

Little Meg came wandering out of her room, dressed in layers and rubbing her eyes. A wail and squeals of protest indicated that Jack was also awake and being changed. Mary scooped the little girl up. "Empty out your toy chest, honeybunch. We're going to need the storage space."

*   *   *

An hour later, they were on the road in a mini-convoy, loaded down with fabric, gardening essentials, non-perishable food, camping stoves and gardening equipment. Mary had the car Bluetooth enabled, keeping in contact with the others. Three more cars and a truck had joined them on the way; other friends with the same idea.

Theo's voice crackled across the speaker. "There's a Bunnings coming up. Saph says that the website lists it as closed. Should we stop?"

Trixie had set up a conference call at the start of the trip. "If we have room, we could use more stuff for gardening and camping."

Ed's voice joined in. "We need to get a lot of that spray that protects glass. Big gardening stakes and as much building material as we can hold, too. I say yes, but be careful."

John's voice settled the matter. "Everyone with kids and full cars, keep going. Everyone with space, branch off and keep together."

Mary still had some room, and her 20- and 30-litre cooking pots could hold small things. She joined the Bunnings team.

*   *   *

The parking lot was deserted, the shop abandoned in enough of a hurry that the staff hadn't done much more than lock the door. A bit of smashed glass later, and Mary was trying to ignore the blaring alarms as she headed for the hardware section. Nails, hammers and saws went into her baskets, along with all the glue she could find.

A growl came from behind her, and she spun to see a shambling corpse, half-rotted already, slowly coming toward her. Mary screamed, the best she could do to warn the others, and grabbed a long-handled mallet, swinging it as hard as she could. Her aim was off, and she hit the neck, but it accomplished the task of sending the zombie's head skimming down the aisle, and its body slumped in place. Mary shouldered the mallet and headed back to the entrance. What she had would need to be enough.

The others joined her, clutching their own supplies. They all scattered to the sides as Mike and Ida came flying down the front aisle from the Garden area. They were perched on laden trolleys, careening wildly but somehow staying upright. The check-out counter halted their flight with an unpleasant-sounding '*crunch*', and Ida climbed down, looking shaken. "There's a bunch of them out the back. Time's up, we need to go."

*   *   *

After commandeering one of the Bunnings Delivery trucks, already mostly loaded when the zombies found them, it only took another hour after that to reach the two neighbouring farms that had been offered as sanctuary. Located in sparsely-populated areas, there were larger towns nearby, but not for kilometers, and not so large that they would produce an insurmountable horde.

Mary had barely put the brakes on her car before she was surrounded by other survivors, helping her unload. Steve, the owner of the farm, submitted to a tight hug. "How are you at inventory? We need a group to start making lists."

Mary grinned in a self-deprecating way, relieved. "Much better than I am at building things, plus I have spare notebooks and pens."

One group of people were keeping the small children out of the way, while others were organising the increasing stockpiles of supplies. A third group were already working on a wall around the perimeter of the main property. Mary went to join the organisers, recognising several friends, leaving the random helpers to unpack.

Right, first, a list of everything they had, then divide and cross reference that into categories. She handed out notebooks and pens. They could do this...

Fighting Under The Mistletoe

Someone challenged me to write a parody of popular Christmas songs, to combat the endless repeats that start before we're even past Halloween! This is the first.

Someone's halls are getting decked

Fa la la la la la la la la

'Tis the season to get wrecked

Fa la la la la la la la la

Don we now our combat gear

Fa la la la la la la la la

Flyt and fight, farewell the year

Fa la la la la la la la la

See the halls ablaze before us

Fa la la la la la la la la

Duck and cover or join the ruckus

Fa la la la la la la la la

Singing, brawling, all together

Fa la la la la la la la la

Get kicked out into the weather

Fa la la la la la la la la

The year behind is nearly finished

fa la la la la la la la la

Say goodbye with a violent skirmish

fa la la la la la la la la

Bumps and bruises, harsh contusions

fa la la la la la la la la

Drink toasts amid the loud confusion

fa la la la la la la la la

Deck the Halls and not your family

fa la la la la la la la la

Just sit back and swig that brandy

fa la la la la la la la la

It's nearly over, til next year

fa la la la la la la la la

So grit your teeth and fake some cheer

fa la la la la la la la la!

A Hero's Day Off

A request from a fan, that unfortunately came after I published the book of side stories for my Hero Trilogy. So, it's going here instead.

Jason, codename Phoenix, glared down at the kitchen table in full uniform and wondered, not for the first time, how he had allowed himself to be talked into this.

Well, that wasn't entirely true. He knew exactly how he had been talked into this, because it happened like clockwork. One of the twins thought it was a good idea, convinced the rest of their Superhero team, and Jason got dragged along for the ride because he didn't want to fuel media rumours of trouble in the ranks.

Fates knew how the Press got an 'Impending breakdown' out of a mild disagreement, but it never stopped them in the past. It didn't matter that the five close friends were the furthest thing from parting ways over whether or not they made a YouTube Video; if the tabloids couldn't find something to be scandalised over, they would make something up. It was one of the many reasons that Jason did his best to avoid them in the first place.

Well, it was too late to back out now. Evanna, better known by the somewhat misleading code-name of Tsunami, finished meddling with the tripod camera and gave him a thumbs-up. Jason was just glad that no-one could see him rolling his eyes behind the bird-like mask. "Welcome to basic domestics, a how-to guide for all of those Heroes and Civilians who didn't get to experience Home Economics, and are - oh, Shadow, seriously?"

Shadow Queen, better known to him as Riona and the instigator of this whole mess, scowled at him from behind the camera. "What? It's accurate!"

Jason rolled his eyes again. "It makes me sound like a third-rate talk show host!"

Melissa, known to an adoring public as Winter Queen and to Jason and Riona as the third member of their romantic triad, giggled off-screen. "Fine, we'll do the talking and you can stand there and look pretty."

She and Riona flanked him before he could bolt, and Jason tried to focus on the task in front of him. It was a good thing he adored them so much.

Riona smiled at the camera, the bright, cheerful grin that suggested she was enjoying a laugh at someone else's expense. "As we were saying, welcome to Basic Domestics, for those of you who were never taught how to manage your own home, and are sick of living off take-out."

Melissa elbowed Jason before he could make a sarcastic comment, smoothly picking up the lines. "Now, it's probably not your fault - we all know that Villains have the worst sense of timing - but you're going to have to learn at some point, so why not now?"

The final member of their team, Morgan, otherwise known as Riona's chaotic other-half or Naiad, directed the camera briefly out the window and into the garden. Specifically, the box-garden of herbs and the vegetable patch. "If you're like us, and keep missing the farmer's market because Supervillains have lousy timing, you might want to think about scheduled delivery, or growing your own, especially if you're on good terms with a plant elemental."

Evanna chipped in, the fact that she was off-screen concealing her broad smirk. "Isn't that cheating?"

Jason glowered. "Do you want a cooked dinner tonight, or another round of delivery drivers playing 'Guess-The-Suburb-While-The-Food-Gets-Cold'? Besides, Demeter owes us a favour, and a vegetable garden is easier than waiting for an opportunity for them to save us."

Riona interjected before Evanna could shoot back a comment about the statistical likelihood of that happening, "Silence in the peanut gallery! Now, today we are making a simple garlic bread, which goes with most dishes, but especially pasta or soup. If you have a specific dish you'd like us to make, please comment below.

Melissa opened the window as one of Riona's shadow constructs leapt through, carrying a clove of garlic and a few sprigs of rosemary. Riona quickly peeled and crushed the garlic, handing Jason half a stick of butter. Resigning himself to the inevitable, Jason dropped it into a bowl, heating the dish with his powers. "Traditionally, oil was used, but butter is an acceptable substitute. For those of you who can't control fire, either leave the butter at room temperature for about half an hour, or microwave in ten-second intervals until you reach the desired softness. Once you've done that, mix in the garlic and rosemary."

Melissa turned on the oven while Riona sliced the bread. "Pretty much any bread can be used for this, depending on what your preference is, but you want to make sure that everyone has the equivalent of three-quarters of a sandwich worth of bread. The oven temperature should be high enough to make the bread crispy without burning it."

Jason had made garlic bread a thousand times, and the rhythm was familiar. "Now, spread the - oh, come on!"

The alarm that signaled a Villain attack went off, and Naiad and Tsunami vanished upstairs to grab their costumes. Shadow Queen vaulted out the window, calling for Nocturne, while Winter Queen pulled up the mission details. Jason shoved the tray of bread into the oven, put the timer on for ten minutes on low heat, and shut the door. "I swear Villains do this on purpose! We'll be back to show you how to make soup."

He joined his team-mates on Nocturne, and the dragon took off.

*   *   *

After the Villains - a bunch of would-be bank-robbers - had been hauled away to cool their heels in a cell overnight, they wrapped up the video, posted it, and settled down to dinner.

Halfway through, Jason's communicator buzzed with a message from the Admin

Sidekick who kept an eye on what was being said about them online. "Just so you know, my next performance review will include negotiating a raise."

He tried not to laugh, ignoring the twins giggling, and switched to speaker-mode. "You're worth it. The initial reaction is positive?"

The sound that come over the device could have been a quiet growl, or maybe it was just the connection. "I'm going to have to create a new data-base just to process the number of dish requests! There are three new offers of marriage just for you!" Melissa laughed outright, the chain that held her wedding ring making a brief appearance from under her shirt as her head tilted back. "Plus five more for the Queens, and more food-based euphemisms than I knew existed! Who knew the ability to cook was so highly prized these days?"

Riona coughed on a bite of her soup as she tried to swallow and laugh at the same time. "I suppose we can expect another irritated call from the council in the morning, then."

The glare from their media liaison was almost tangible through the airwaves. "What do you think? They've spent the last week trying to share the attention around some of the other teams, and you just knocked all of them back down again when this went viral."

Jason couldn't help a satisfied grin. Angering the council was dangerous; for all that they were stuck two decades in the past and spent more time maintaining the status quo than doing anything productive, they were still powerful. On the other hand, after all the crap the Superhero Council had pulled in regards to their team, there was a certain amount of pleasure to be found in making their lives difficult. Riona smirked as she put down her spoon. "Make a short-list of the most popular requests, and we'll go through it from easiest to hardest. Don't worry about the council."

As was frequently the case, Morgan elaborated on what her twin neglected to explain. "They can't censor us without providing justification and evidence, and as things stand, they don't have anything that we can't spin into a PR nightmare for the entire department, not to mention a dangerous precedent that even their most hardcore supporters would think twice about."

Evanna propped her chin on her hand, smiling at her girlfriend, "If popularity was a crime, there are a lot of teams who would need to be worried, and the only complaints against us so far are from a bunch of school-kids who had to actually sit their exams because we wrap our Epic Battles up quickly, and they'd been counting on a protracted fight to delay them enough that they'd have to re-sit at a later date."

Melissa laughed, "Well, if that's the worst result we get from our battles, I'm happy. Perhaps one day we'll even manage to have the full day off.

Stages of Grief

Written shortly after my twin died, this popped up again when I was cleaning out my Trash folder. Given the upcoming anniversary of her passing, it seemed fitting.

An ocean of tears, a well of sorrow,

Reluctance to be forced to face tomorrow.

Loss of your family, of a lover or friend,

A pain that seemingly has no end.

A sister's grief, a mother's cry,

Both unwilling to say goodbye.

The Heavens weep, a misery of weather,

Reflection of wishing for more time together

Stages of grief, a friend's denial

A son's anger rages in a deepening spiral

A twin's useless bargaining, a lover's
depression

A brother's acceptance, the final concession

A breakdown, a crisis, Animosity too,

Or spiritual faith, "They'll be born anew."

Arguments over conflicting beliefs,

Yet united as one in sharing their grief

Time eases all wounds, and Agony fades,

To Quiet Remembrance when visiting graves.

With us in spirit, and never truly gone,

We think of them fondly, as life goes on.

Deathworlds

From one of the many, many 'Humans are Space Orcs/Earth is Space Australia' threads on Tumblr. Humans might not be the most dangerous thing around, but we're resilient, as well as spiteful and contrary.

The Aliens wanted us to submit, and imprisoned the ones who wouldn't. They were prepared for human rebellion. It was the rest of the native fauna that they should have worried about...

Their prisoner/guide would be much easier to tolerate, the captain thought, if she wasn't so clearly enjoying their suffering.

Solaris 3 - "Earth", as the natives called it - was unmistakably a Deathworld of epic proportions. The captain of the A"vaar'i might have even called it a Hellworld, if not for the knowledge that he would get demoted for doing so. How the primitive humans had survived for so long was a mystery.

The captain looked again at the guide, a female of what he had been told was average age for the species. She was knowledgeable about the monsters they faced, at least, and as a bonus, shared the invaders distaste for the more unpleasant ones. However, it seemed that the wildlife was not the only problem they faced.

How was the human still standing in heat of 27°C or more? The squadron was having to rest every half-hour, to give their cooling units, the only things keeping them from being cooked alive, time to recharge. Certainly, the human had been drinking more water than usual, and had stripped down to a thin, single layer, but otherwise she seemed largely unbothered by the infernal heat.

Unable to resist, the captain approached the human as the squadron all-but-collapsed at their next rest break. "How do you stand it?"

The human finished drinking and moved to refill their water-bottle. "You may need to be more specific. If you mean your general existence, I'm only going along with this to avoid being murdered."

Humans were so dramatic! She would merely be dissected and studied to further enhance their knowledge of Solaris 3. Perhaps parts of her adaptive DNA might be cloned and mutated for their own use, but nothing a healthy A"vaar'i could not survive. "No, the heat."

To his surprise, she laughed. "This? Oh, mate, you ain't seen nothing yet! Just wait until we hit high summer! It gets all the way up to the 40's, then."

The captain was glad that his helmet hid him from the human's sight. It would not do for the human to see the expression of horror he wore. "Surely you jest."

She shook her head, some of that insufferable cheer back in her voice when she heard the dismay in his. "Nope. Be glad we're in the plains and not the desert. That's even worse."

Worse? It could get worse than this? The captain tried not to let panic at the very idea. "How do you stand it?"

She shrugged. "We didn't get to be the dominant species by being the biggest and strongest. We survived by adaptation, by the ability to withstand extreme temperatures, to shape the environment to our needs and to outlast the creatures we hunted."

Something about her tone caught the captain's attention. "Outlast?"

The human bared her teeth in what the briefing said was a smile, though there was little friendly intent behind it. "I'm not even in peak health, and I can walk for hours, even in this heat. We used to follow our prey until they could flee no more and died of exhaustion. Or we killed them."

The captain had a very bad feeling, confirmed by the human's next words. "I've been watching. You can't stand extreme temperatures like us, and even in temperate weather, you have to rest frequently, for longer and longer periods. If we'd thought to try pursuit predation from the start, your invasion would never have succeeded."

Her smile became vicious, like those of the thrice-dreaded tiger, and she leaned in. "I've been leading you in circles for the past week, and I'm well-rested. I could kill you, but I'm not feeling quite that merciful. Bye!"

*　　*　　*

They chased her, of course, but to no avail. The human walked at a brisk pace, for hours on end. Even moving at full speed during their mobile intervals, they caught only glimpses of her before they were forced to stop and rest. By the second day, they had lost not only the human, but any idea of where they were.

The human had been right; it would have been mercy to kill them.

The Soldier

A soldier once marched off to war, halberd held up high

His mail and coat were bright and new, his shiny boots were spry

He had no fear of hurt or death, dreams of glory filled his mind

The bards would surely sing his name, oh, the adventures he would find!

He marched alone, o'er cobbled path, no army yet in sight,

No foeman near, no robber band, no enemy to
fight

Two sheep jostled for a grazing patch, and a cat
it eyed a crow,

But peaceful was the countryside, under
summer sun's bright glow

Well the years marched on, in double time, and
the soldier marched apace

He had met farmers, merchants, squires and a
knight armed with a mace

But no war he found, and conflicts few, for a
wise head bore the crown

No chance for he, a lowly guard, to wage battle
and win renown.

A soldier once marched home from war, his
halberd held his pack

His coat was patched and dark with rust, and
heavy on his back

His boots were worn, his helmet served as a
nest for swallows four

Just one more bridge and then he'd find the
navy at its moor!

Christmas Eve Alone

Someone challenged me to write a parody of popular Christmas songs, to combat the endless repeats that start in every shopping centre and public space before we're even past Halloween! This is number two.

Away in a dark pub, no beer for to drink

Nativity carols (We messed the lyrics we think).

The houses are lit up, my night-vision's screwed,

The Holy silhouette is two T-Rex, a chainsaw their feud.

You cannot un-see it, you curse me out loud,

I laugh at your outrage, in a drunken cloud.

No visiting family, couldn't get time off work

I sit in this bar now, proclaiming my boss is a jerk.

I am Scrooge pre-redemption, I cry humbug today

Expectations and food waste, there are still bills to pay.

See the hungry and homeless, while you feast warm and dry

Forget those in need, for Christmas is nigh.

From the Imagination

Thanks to Lucy from my online Fantasy group, who make a One Ring reference to her draft, and was promptly bombarded with "One Book..." poems. This was my contribution.

Three drafts for Fantasy High

Seven for Sword and Sorcery and Stone

Nine for Grimdark where everyone dies

One for the editor to check and hone

From the imagination where ideas lie.

One book to deep enthrall

One book to write, then

One book, on pages scrawl,

And in a cover bind them!

From the imagination where ideas lie

It's Our Shared Dream

One of my camp-mates at Pennsic mentioned how much they hate the song "It's A Small World, After All", so, naturally, about half of the rest of us started singing it. Potential stabbing (with blunted rapiers) was prevented by the Widow Montoya starting to filk it, instead, and giving me ideas...

It's a world of combat, a world of steel,

You get cut down, go to Res Point to heal.

From Crown Tourney to war, it's combat we adore,

It's our dream in the SCA!

It's the dream of SCA!

It's the dream of SCA!

It's the dream of SCA!

It is our shared dream!

It's a world of service, and a world of art,

Volunteering and research, we all play a part.

Jack- or Jill-of-all-trades, Pelican's accolades,

Choose your dream in the SCA!

It's the dream of SCA!

It's the dream of SCA!

It's the dream of SCA!

It is our shared dream!

Once

*The result of a prompt at one of my writers' meet ups. **"I never stood a chance, did I?" / "That's the sad part - you did, once."** I don't know that this will ever become anything more than the fifteen-minute flash fiction is it, but that's writing for you.*

I sat on the large bed, somehow all the larger for the knowledge of what could have been, but now never would be.

I understood, now, why people had spoken of crossroads as a dangerous place, something to be feared. I stood at a crossroads in my life now, choices that were equally terrifying and rewarding before me, and I didn't want to make them. Not that life had ever really paid attention to what I wanted. Why start now?

My dream job, that came with the tiny requirement of moving across the country, eased by company housing but complicated by the fact that you could only bring family or de facto partners with you.

My boyfriend was always complaining about how there were no jobs to be found, how he wanted to get out of the small town we grew up in, but now that we had the chance…

I expected him to be happy at the opportunity, or if he couldn't be happy, to at least consider a long-distance relationship, or even making things official, however we preferred. More fool me.

Moving in together was apparently "too much of a commitment" for him, but wanting me to turn down a once-in-a-lifetime offer was no big deal and I was "Over-reacting". It's not like I was asking him to marry me, just to make a solid commitment. I thought he wanted to get away, experience life somewhere new!

Apparently, only if it was on his terms. Now, he was making what should be an occasion worth celebrating all about him. I finished folding my clothes and stood up, walking over to the cupboard to pull down my suitcase.

He scowled. "I never stood a chance, did I?"

I bit back my first three responses. Why did he think I asked him to come with me in the first place? I had thought it would be an opportunity for us! Until he decided that having a girlfriend who would be the obvious breadwinner was 'emasculating', or some such shit.

I should have been upset at our break-up, but all I felt was resignation. This had been a long time coming, overdue even. I just hadn't wanted to admit it.

I sighed, a tiny part of me wishing for a return to the way things had been, before he had disappointed me so much, and a larger part knowing that I couldn't go back. "That's the sad part. You did, once."

Bloody (Furious)

Mary

From an online prompt, "It's fun to chant 'Bloody Mary' into your sideview mirror three times and watch her jog to try to catch up"

Written more to make my girlfriend laugh than anything, I liked it enough to include it.

I sat in my car, waiting for the lights to change so I could turn onto the highway. The cars going in the opposite direction slowed, suggesting that the lights were about to change. Perfect.

I glanced at my side-view mirror; the timing had to be exact, or I would be in a lot of trouble. Also pain, probably. "Bloody Mary, Bloody Mary, Bloody Mary."

The lights changed as the mirror distorted. A pale, gaunt young woman with lank hair emerged as I pressed the accelerator. Her expression changed from placid menace to extreme irritation as she had to dodge a truck, a startled windscreen washer panning for change, and other hazards of mid-day city traffic.

Funny, the feared apparition was a lot less terrifying when she was red and puffing, the hem of her ragged dress lifted so as not to trip over it while she chased after my car.

I'd probably suffer for this later, but it was so, so worth it.

*   *   *

The next time I tried was on a train. Someone on the station was fixing their make-up in a hand mirror, which was apparently vastly more important than letting people get on and off public transport. She was lucky that one guy was in a wheelchair; he'd looked ready to kick her onto the tracks when the wheelchair ramp had to be angled sideways for him to get off without running her over. Luckily, his carer had wheeled him away before he got the chance.

That just made what I was about to do with that mirror all the more sweet.

The angle at which I was leaning out of the train window was probably going to leave bruises, and I had to be ready to pull my head back in a hurry, but it was better than risking the glass as a reflective surface/passageway from the Beyond. I fixed my attention on the mirror as the whistle blew. "Bloody Mary, Bloody Mary, Bloody Mary."

The person fixing their face paint - seriously, hadn't they heard that make-up was supposed to be natural unless you were a clown? - screamed and dropped the mirror as the spook in question clawed her way out of the handheld mirror. It required a bit of a wiggle at two points - feminine curves could be a hindrance when trying to get through a confined space - and the train was safely picking up speed as Mary looked around and spotted me.

She screamed even louder than the person whose mirror I'd hijacked, though probably more in rage and frustration than in fear, and sprinted after the train, leaving the mirror on the ground and the person who had been holding it a rocking, gibbering wreck. My carriage was passing the edge of the platform at that point, so her efforts were futile. Of course, I'd timed it that way.

I waved cheekily at her rapidly-shrinking figure... and had to yank my hand back inside before I broke it on the edge of a tunnel.

Still totally worth it.

*　　*　　*

The third time is the charm, and I was having far too much fun with this to quit now.

This time, I was on a ferry between Wellington and Picton, the harbour towns of the North and South Islands of New Zealand, and had just found out that even massive, car-carrying ferries have side mirrors.

Even if it didn't work, we were nearly at the dock, so there were plenty of places for me to hide from an angry spectre until I got off. Plus, kids had been running up and down this deck, yelling, for at least the past hour. The other passengers stretching their legs outside were aggressively ignoring anything from this level. No-one would notice a thing. Worst case scenario, the pint-sized howling terrors would get something to scream about.

I leaned against the railing, enjoying the wind in my hair and the smell of salt and brine. I looked over to the mirrors, just barely close enough for me to see my reflection. "Bloody Mary, Bloody Mary, Bloody Mary."

She started to emerge, with a howl of triumph. (That was new - I must have been even more annoying than I thought.) The ferry jolted, like the helmsman had just received a shock and yanked the wheel, and Mary Worth's glee turned to a shriek as she fell out of the mirror and plummeted several dozen feet into the harbour below.

A few people on the lower decks looked up from their conversations or reading material at the loud splash. The brat who had been sneaking up behind random people, in order to scream and scare them, burst into tears and ran back to their parents, who had been pointedly Not Noticing the brat's antics.

A voice came from beside me, the good-looking stranger I'd been casually eyeing as I weighed my odds of success if I made a move. "Nice.

Wanna see if they're still serving drinks at the bar?"

Ok, giving Bloody Mary a soaking would never not be worth it, but this was an unexpected bonus. "A red snapper sounds lovely."

A Red Snapper was a variation on the Bloody Mary cocktail. My potential date laughed and led the way.

*   *   *

Of course, my cunning, brilliant plan to cheat doom was all bound to go wrong eventually.

The first warning sign should have been when I used the story to chat up a pretty girl at a Halloween bash. Bragging about stupid and/or dangerous exploits to impress a disinterested girl is always dangerous; chick-flicks should have taught me that much. She'd been looking into her phone camera, trying to get a good

Selfie angle, when I sidled up to her, and it was not resting on the table between us.

The girl herself wasn't quite so into the Halloween spirit that she was willing to believe me without question. I reached for her phone (the dangerously-raised eyebrow should have been another warning sign). She moved it out of my reach, and I backed off, looking toward the bar. "Look, I'll show you. Bloody Mary - argh!"

I had barely finished the first repetition before she came screaming out of the iPhone. "I WILL EAT YOUR SOUL, YOU WRETCH!"

I'd been looking at the mirror over the bar (whose tender had insisted on showing him my ID, even though I was well over the age limit), but my face was also just visible in the pretty girl's phone. Said pretty girl was also remarkably unphased by my screaming. Bloody Mary came out claws first, using my face as an anchor point to pull herself the rest of the way. Then she got to work.

All of those times I said I wanted some cool scars to impress the ladies? *THIS WAS NOT WHAT I MEANT!*

I fell to the floor, groaning, the other partygoers either not noticing or thinking that it was part of the evening's entertainment. Her fearsome visage gentled, looking almost creepy-attractive, as she glanced at the girl I'd been flirting with. "I appreciate your help. The wretch was always prepared by the third repetition, but with you saying the first two..."

The pretty girl smiled. "Likewise. Want to hang with me for a bit before you go back? You won't stand out here."

Bloody Mary - even more bloody than usual tonight - considered briefly, then nodded. "Just let me dispose of this one. I won't be a moment."

Lifting me up like I weighed less than a doll, she somehow started stuffing me into the reflective surface of a beer glass.

Oh, no. Look, I can take scars, I can take a probably well-deserved beating, but being stuck in a beer glass for eternity? Yeah, I'll nope right out of that, thanks.

Bloody Mary hadn't got that memo, or didn't care, because her very vindictive grin was the last thing I saw before a clear but very solid barrier overtook my view. The pretty girl - I hadn't even scored her name! - set my glass on the edge of the table, and led Bloody Mary onto the dance floor. She'd been dressed as a Greek goddess, and it was only now that I noticed the flail tucked into her belt, next to a long dagger.

Nemesis, the goddess of Vengence and Retribution, dancing with a vengeful spirit. How very fitting. Part of me wondered if it really was just a costume, or if I'd spent the past ten minutes annoying an actual goddess. If Bloody Mary was real, why not other folklore?

The famous couplet sprung into my mind, trapped in my glassy hell, just as someone bumped the table and the glass started to fall. I decided that it needed an update, or at least an extension. If Hell had the monopoly on scorned women, and Heaven on love turned to hate, then Purgatory must be the wrath of a woman pushed beyond her limits.

A pity that I'd learned that bit of wisdom too late.

Ice Eyes

Written for an acquaintance in some of my online writing groups, after they asked for help with a poem for the novel they were writing. Struggling artists aren't exactly rolling in cash to pay for commissions, so we agreed that I could add it to my collections and he would credit me with the poem.

His arms were strong, yet useless hung

as he gazed o'er the field of shattered green

A feud like those of which the poets sung

turned friend to foe, all hope of truce unseen.

A voice called his name, his faithful second

he turned to look at his waiting men

No doubt they felt, whatever Fate reckoned

Spirit shaking, he could not fail them.

"My Lord, can we win?" He does not know,

But raises his sword and banners high.

For kinfolk and homeland, he cannot fail,

No matter how many will die.

Horns ring out, their fatal song

As clear as his ice-blue eyes

Two armies clash, both right and both wrong

Under blood-red, smoke-filled skies

Dearest friends fall, beside hated foe

He fights on with tears in his eyes

Defiantly roars, inspires his men so

Not to make worthless their sacrifice.

Night falls cold, on a silent field

The battle and the field are theirs

A price too high, though Peace it yields

The knowledge does not stop his tears.

Escape

Another Tumblr writing prompt, which became another short story for my Superhero series.

"It's rather nice to be on the other side of this for once." The villain grinned down at the incapacitated hero, slamming the cell door shut. "Let's see if you're as crafty as I am. My escape record was, oh, forty minutes? Let's find out yours."

Morgan, better known as Naiad, folded her arms and glared at Houdini's Bane. She could appreciate the originality of the code-name, but right now it wasn't helpful. Until now, he'd been just a very talented escape artist whenever the assorted Hero teams managed to arrest him, and the other teams had laughed it off when Winter Queen suggested that it might have a double meaning.

The Guardians were one of the few teams who hadn't had the embarrassment of Houdini's

Bane escaping before he could be turned over to police, mostly by keeping a very firm grip on him the entire time. Apparently, he'd taken it personally, and decided that kidnapping one of them in turn was only fair.

Luckily, they'd planned for it. Houdini had no idea about the tiny marble that Naiad had slipped into his pocket, or the tracking beacon in her mask. Or the fact that it wasn't the first time she'd been kidnapped, even if the people kidnapping her the first few times had called it *'removal from undue bad influence'*.

(The Pied Piper had disagreed, and eviscerated the culprit in court. Three public defence lawyers had taken emergency medical leave rather than be assigned that case and face the angry Villainess across the courtroom.)

Houdini's Bane may or may not have designed his imitation prison after the Supermax designed to hold Powered Villains, but he probably hadn't considered the benefits of teamwork, or that Heroes might actually bother with planning for being captured. In fairness, most Heroes didn't, and it had been only a few years since Heroes stopped ignoring their Sidekick's warnings about a situation being a trap. With their mixed upbringing, Naiad, Shadow Queen and Phoenix tended to be the exception to stereotypical Hero behaviour.

From the control room, there was a loud yell, the sound of a body crashing into or over a solid object, and a '*whoosh*' noise. Most people - unless they checked the registry - thought that Tsunami was named for invisibility or stealth powers, rather than her actual ability to turn into a ball. The Guardians tended to encourage that belief, if only because it resulted in Villains and other criminals planning the wrong defense against her.

Naiad grinned, and sat back in her cell, enjoying the sound of something bouncing off several walls, accompanied by more frustrated shouting. Houdini's Bane came into view again, trapped inside the kind of giant inflatable hamster ball that Naiad had seen beach-goers playing in recently. The keys to her cell were bouncing on the top of the ball, with Houdini's Bane trying to get them, and Tsunami's ball form careening wildly off the walls to stop him.

Tsunami flung herself to one side, sending the keys sliding off to just outside Naiad's cell, and then promptly transformed herself into a giant steel ball. A metallic 'clang' and more swearing, this time rather slurred, came from inside, followed by a 'thunk'. Naiad sniggered, unlocking her cell as Tsunami changed back, leaving Houdini's Bane unconscious on the floor. "What was that?"

Her girlfriend smirked, clapping power-restraining cuffs on the Villain. "Antique Parisian Sewer Ball. They're made of semi-hard plastic, these days, but metal suited my purpose better."

Naiad slung the Villain over her shoulder as sirens sounded from outside, heralding the police arriving. "You didn't happen to time it, did you?"

Tsunami adjusted her mask. "Ten minutes, but maybe don't spread it around? I'd rather not have Houdini's Bane spreading my powers around, much less the jokes I'd get."

Naiad and Shadow Queen still had to suffer far too many comments about their speculated love lives, and with Tsunami being a firm batter for the home team, comments about 'having a Villain inside her' would be even less welcome than usual. Naiad sighed, "It's really telling that even Superheroines have to deal with Dudebros on the internet making inappropriate comments."

Phoenix, who had been the closest when their trackers went off, walked in just in time to hear her. "Acid gets out next week, we can always send him over and call in an anonymous tip about drugs."

Naiad patted him on the shoulder as Tsunami grinned. "This is why you're my favourite brother."

He rolled his eyes, "Foster-brother, and Michel doesn't count, so I'm pretty sure that I'm also your only brother."

Naiad sniggered again, "Practical Brother-in-law, too, since you're sleeping with my sister. Eek!"

A fiery kitten pounced at her foot, dissipating with a wave of Phoenix's hand. Tsunami laughed, getting ready to knock Houdini's Bane out again as the Villain groaned and started to stir. "You had that one coming, dearest. Now, Hero Faces for the cameras and let's hope that the Supermax Prison can keep this one for more than five minutes this time."

Phoenix groaned; at least half of the magazine photos of him had an annoying focus on his bare, sculpted arms lately. He didn't care how hot the weather was, or how much his two girlfriends appreciated it show; he intended to go back to a full-cover jacket as soon as he had enough downtime to sew the sleeves back on. "Get him transferred straight to one on the other side of the continent. They can deal with him for a change."

Naiad raised an eyebrow, "Are we allowed to send our Villains to other jurisdictions?"

"By the time the Superhero Council finds out, will they be able to stop us?" Winter Queen appeared, slipping an arm around Phoenix's waist. Naiad didn't object, she had adjusted to her twin being part of a Triad long ago. "The worst they can do is have him transferred back, and then we're no worse off than we are now. Shadow is collecting his data for study, by the way."

Naiad's twin emerged, a large bag of data chips carried by a few of her shadow constructs. "I'm making some of the Council Admin deal with these; you'd think a Villain classified as Dangerously Intelligent would go for higher storage USBs, rather than a dozen low-storage ones."

Winter Queen wrapped her other arm around Shadow Queen as they headed for the exit, Phoenix catching Houdini's Bane as he tried to sneak off, an ice-ball to the head sending him back to the land of the unconscious. "Villains rarely make sense, my heart. I know it's my turn to make dinner, but does anyone object to take-out tonight? I'm buggered."

Flashing lights blinded them as they stepped out of the makeshift "prison", paparazzi cameras and police lights alike. Tsunami looked like she was seriously considering turning back into a marble so she could skip the press conference. Naiad sighed. "Let's get through the interviews, and you can call on the way home."

Whitechapel Justice

From yet another writing prompt, this one speculating that the reason Jack the Ripper was never found was because a gang of angry prostitutes got to him first, and didn't bother with arrests.

The shadowed figure walked through the streets on silent feet, as though they were barely more substantial than the foggy mist that blanketed the city.

A body lay on the cobblestones behind them, horribly mutilated. They hadn't made the worthless whore's death a quick one. She didn't deserve such mercy; none of them did. Neither would the victims yet to come, and of those there would be many.

They deserved their fate, all of them. Plagues on society, a stain against the name of all good, hardworking folk that they tempted away from the moral path. Their deaths were practically a civil service, one that the figure was honoured to perform.

The figure looked up at the sound of footsteps, melting back into the shadows as a patrol walked by. They increased their pace, though not more than any other hurrying home after dark.

Just in time; the sound of a whistle shattered the silence of the night, followed by shouts of alarm. The figure joined the crowds of spectators who came out of taverns and houses to see what the commotion was about.

They would stay just long enough to allay suspicion, and lay low for a few weeks.

It was only a stay of execution. Annie Chapman would have company soon enough.

The Prostitutes who plied their trade in the streets of Whitechapel didn't have a guild, like most of the other trades did.

Some thought this unfair, as they were the world's oldest profession, but all agreed that the Mayor and other civic officials would never approve making a Prostitute's Guild official. They barely tolerated the trade as it was, and only under the reasoning that it would find a way to exist no matter what. If the sex trade was going to exist, better that it happen semi-openly, where the workers could be taxed like everyone else, rather than in the shadows. Taxes and fines could only be collected if the crime was discovered, after all.

What the Prostitutes did have, was an informal gathering in a boarding house that doubled as a bordello on nights when the weather made the streets an impractical place to work. No sane man wanted to walk home in trousers and underclothes soaked by rain, or catch a chill from biting winter cold, but the women of Whitechapel still had to earn a living.

The day was crisp but clear, and the boarders were all out at their jobs, allowing the women of Whitechapel to gather without interruption. Mrs Smythe, the proprietress, passed around battered cups filled with tea. The leaves were used, of course, all that she could afford in quantity, but it was still a rare treat for those seated around the tables.

At the head of the room, guiding the meeting as they did their little community, sat the Aunts.

An eclectic bunch, the Aunts consisted of those too old to be active (or attractive to clients) but experienced enough to mentor and guide those lost and new to the profession. These kindly elders were mixed with a scattering of women whose indelicate pursuits had tended in a different direction. Namely, the fighting arts.

Fondly nicknamed the Streetstalkers, they patrolled the streets where the fine, brave officers of Scotland Yard would not go, or did not care to practice too much vigilance. Gangs who saw streetwalkers as an easy target, housewives who found out where their husbands had been, and with whom, men who were looking for an outlet for their anger at their own circumstances... all learned their lesson at deceptively slender hands. Few made such a mistake twice, and those few exceptions never got the chance to repeat their error a third time.

A final two women hurried in, Miss Wilcox and Miss Lucas, who discreetly financed their studies at the Nightingale School for Nurses via their night-time work in Mrs Smythe's back room. They were vital to the Council, healing the injuries that were an inevitable part of life on the streets, and in one or two rare cases, taking care of the bodies that resulted from the Streetstalkers admonishments.

Mrs Smythe sat the newcomers down and called the meeting to order. "You're all aware of why we're here, yes?"

Aunt Sarah, who rarely moved from her rooms these days, with the cold weather nipping at her ancient bones, nodded gravely. "Martha, Mary Ann and Annie. Murdered, poor loves, and by someone who enjoyed it."

They all knew better to mention how Aunt Sarah would know. She had been the first Streetstalker, and had widowed herself when her husband raised his hand to her one time too many. Many of them had known men like that, and chosen the danger of the streets over the danger that waited at home.

Aunt Gertrude, the current head of the Streetstalkers and Aunt Sarah's protegee and prized pupil, nodded. "They've arrested someone for Annie Chapman's murder. My informant with the Yard says that he has an alibi, and the witness who actually saw him, Mrs Long, saw two men but only identified one."

Mrs Smythe looked startled, possibly at the idea that Scotland Yard would have arrested anyone. "Do they know who was arrested?"

Aunt Gertrude nodded gravely, "A hairdresser, yesterday. They brought in old Leather Apron himself, John Pizer, a week yesterday." She waved away the chorus of grumbles and groans, "Yes, any one of us could have identified him, and the Streetstalkers have warned him off already, but he was elsewhere when Annie was murdered. We'll talk to Mrs Long and see if we can't get a better description off her and the other witness."

Miss Lucas shook her blonde head sadly. "Is there a way to get hold of a coroner's report?

We can take a look and narrow down the possible methods used."

Aunt Sarah shook her head. "We need more than that. This killer has a taste for our blood, though whether they have rhyme or reason, or just hold an extreme view of us that most of Society shares, I cannot say. Until this is resolved, no-one goes on the streets alone, and preferably not without the company of a Streetstalker."

Aunt Gertrude backed her up, "The guild dues can pay for a night at a Poorhouse, for those who need it. Streetstalkers, when you're not on duty, I want you working on finding this killer."

Mrs Smythe nodded in agreement. "I'll be open after-hours, for those who need the coin. If the Watch can't end this, then we will."

It would later be said that arresting the Ripper was too much for even the most dedicated and ambitious man.

Fortunately for all concerned, the Streetstalkers were ambitious for a time when Sex Workers could ply their trade in safety, and very, very dedicated to taking down anyone who threatened that.

A body sank into the waters of the Thames, sinking beneath the waves as the current carried it out to sea. The Women of Whitechapel bore silent witness to the killer's fate, and just as silently dispersed. They would mourn their sisters, keeping them alive in memory, but Work never truly ended, and they still had to make a living.

The Ripper wasn't the first to meet such a fate, nor were they likely be the last.

For now, though, the danger had passed, and life went on.

About The Author

Natasja has been writing since a very young age, though those notebooks have been lost in the Old Schoolbooks Cupboard and (hopefully) will never see the light of day.

Most of her stories, published or otherwise, began life as conversations with friends that sparked an idea that grew into a story or poem.

Her publishing adventures started with poems and short stories in focus newsletters like ABA and AMBA, and online sites like Readwave, NaNoWriMo and FictionPress, before finally taking a chance with self-publishing.

Natasja Rose lives and works in Sydney, Australia, but travels whenever she can.

Her greatest wish is to visit all the places in the world that inspired her writing as a child and create new stories for new inspirations

Eternity's Invitation

Dealing with her best friend being possessed by the ghost of a star-crossed lover was just the beginning.

Returning to a place where she swore she would never set foot again, Tina Barnes is once again dragged kicking and screaming into the realm of the Supernatural.

At least she has company this time.

In the gripping sequel to 'The Highwayman's Legacy', re-join the usual suspects in a series of ghostly murders that have nothing to do with star-crossed lovers....

And everything to do with destroying anyone who has the potential to stop them.

Book Two of Ghostly Travels
Available in Kindle ebook and Paperback

All You Can Be

Living With Aspergers, by Aspies and those who love them

Asperger's Syndrome affects different people in different ways, from Aspies themselves, to people who have friends or family with the condition.

This is a collection of stories and anecdotes, ranging from the good things about being Aspie, to common coping strategies, to media misrepresentation and how it affects people of all ages and backgrounds.

Being Aspie is far from being all fun and games, but there are definitely far worse things to be.

Available in Kindle ebook and Paperback

All That We Are

The Asexuality Spectrum, or Love Without Sex

We live in a very sexualised society, where sex without love is common, but love without sex seems to shock people.

In this book, we will discuss the spectrum of Asexuality, as viewed by the people who live it. This is a collection of anecdotes, ranging from discovering your sexuality, to common misconceptions and prejudice, and basic definitions of the different terms

Being diverse might come with its problems, but what's the point if you can't be yourself?

Available in Kindle ebook and Paperback

All That I Need
Childfree by Choice

Raising a family is not for everyone.

Whether because of your incompatible lifestyle, personal reasons or general disinterest in small humans, a growing number of people are choosing not to reproduce. This choice is often perceived as incomprehensible to the general, child-having, populace.

Contained within the book are a series of anecdotes from people who have chosen, for one reason or another, not to become parents. Hopefully, it will increase understanding in the community that just because you don't agree with a choice, doesn't make it wrong or invalid.

Book Three of Living Diversity
Available Now in Paperback and Kindle Ebook

The Lost Collection

A place for my poems, short stories and other things that didn't quite merit a book of their own.

You will find short plays for all ages, parody songs, fictional monologues for historical figures, and much more.

Read about Boudicca of the Iceni and the Nika Riots, the woes of an average schoolgirl, the best way to derail a science vs theology debate, and what happens when nursery rhymes go bad.

Whether laughing at comedy or crying over tragedy, this anthology will keep you entertained through to the end.

Available in Kindle ebook and Paperback

The Writing Prompt Collection

Short stories, plus the occasional monologue and poem, inspired by writing prompts.

Read about the night-time protectors, a different take on the gingerbread witch, which industry the Millennial Generation is killing this time, and how to REALLY say it with flowers.

A fun read that will have you laughing, crying and groaning by turns, The Writing Prompt Collection is the latest in a series of Anthologies by Natasja Rose.

Available in Kindle Ebook and Paperback

Cinderella Grows A Spine

Cinderella didn't know exactly what prompted her to break free of the cycle of abuse from her step-mother, but one thing was certain: nothing is ever accomplished by waiting for someone else to magically fix things.

After all, Cinderella was a pretty, educated young lady of high birth and good breeding, and her Step-mother didn't control the world, no matter what the woman thought.

It wasn't like she didn't have options...

In a delightful reinvention of the classic fairytale, Cinderella takes charge of her own destiny, and through the power of friendship, courage and liberal applications of common sense, finds her own Happily Ever After

Book One of Timeless Tales, Modern Morals
Available in Kindle ebook and Paperback

Snow White Learns Stranger Danger

People in Fairytales are far too trusting. But what if they weren't?

Snow White learned at a young age that not everyone has good intentions, and that being a Princess didn't mean that everyone loved her.

There were people who were kind without expecting anything in return, and there probably were old beggar-women who were happy to repay a good deed, but this one was far too insistent about being allowed into the house.

In a unique re-imagining of the Classic Fairytale, Snow White learns the value of friendship, sensible precautions, and a good cast-iron skillet.

Sequel to '*Cinderella Grows a Spine*'.

Book One of Timeless Tales, Modern Morals
Available in Kindle ebook and Paperback

Red Riding Hood and the Stalker

Appearances can be deceiving, but a person's true nature is impossible to fully hide.

Ruby was getting very, very sick of having to hide out at her grandmothers because it was the only place Adrian Wolfe wouldn't follow her. Really, hadn't anyone ever told him that Stalking was not romantic, and that no means no?

A retelling of 'Little Red Riding Hood', in which Stalking because you "can't stay away" is a giant red flag, and the Big Bad Wolf isn't quite so obviously a Villain. Sequel to 'Snow White Learns Stranger Danger'.

Book Three of Timeless Tales, Modern Morals
Available in Kindle ebook and Paperback

Beautiful, Inside and Out

What do you do when your arrogance and pride leaves you alone in the world? Some people lash out, falling deeper and deeper into darkness. Others learn from the experience, and become better for it. Isabella had never realised how much she would regret driving Sophia away, but she knew that before she could change things between them, she would need to change herself.

In a journey of self-discovery, friendship and the occasional scandal, Isabella realises that true beauty is found within, and that loving someone else is no help if you can't love yourself as well.

A 'twisted fairytale' retelling of Beauty and the Beast. Side-story to "Cinderella Grows a Spine" and "Snow White Learns Stranger Danger".

Book Four of Timeless Tales, Modern Morals

Available in Kindle ebook and Paperback

BETWEEN DARKNESS AND LIGHT

It wasn't Jason's fault that his father's Ultimate Sacrifice hadn't resulted in Martyrdom, but in a Villainous reputation.

It wasn't Evanna's fault that she had been in the wrong place at the wrong time, and would up with Superpowers a la toxic waste.

It wasn't Stretch's fault that his teachers focused more on using his powers than on the ethics of doing so.

In a world where Superpowers are common, and those gifted with them a facet of everyday life, the lines between Hero and Villain are not always so easily drawn.

As though being a teenager wasn't hard enough!

Book One of "Two Sides of the Same Coin"

Available in Paperback and Kindle ebook

TO LIGHT THE WAY IN DARKNESS

The first year at the Superhero Academy ended with a lot of changes, but that doesn't mean that the Super-student's problems are over.

Discrimination is still rife in the ranks, and just because things are changing doesn't mean that the underlying problems have gone away. On top of that, there are several of the 'Old Crowd' who are angry at the reluctant Superheroes as the source of all these changes, and want nothing more than to paint them as Villains.

The younger generation will need to step up their game, and keep a constant watch, if they want to survive to graduate.

Book Two of "Two Sides of the Same Coin"
Available in Paperback and Kindle ebook

A CANDLE IN THE NIGHT

A collection of short stories based around the world and characters from the "***Two Sides of the Same Coin***" trilogy.

Read about Alien Invasions begun and ended in ways that will give future historians some very interesting days at the office, how Supervillains formed their on Council, and how DIY costumes aren't always the best idea.

From Villainous backstories, to relationships, these stories will entertain you in the best of ways.

Side Stories from the "Two Sides of the Same Coin" Trilogy

Available in Paperback and Kindle ebook

The Time Traveller's Seamstress

Time Travel is easy. Fitting in while surfing the time-space continuum is harder.

A big part of the Time Agency's success was due to their costuming department, a variety of men and women who made fantastic clothing... and who really wished that the Agents would pay more attention to details like what year and geographical region they were heading to, and the policy on advanced notice for anything pre-1920s. Honestly, do they think all of that hand-stitched embroider and beading is easy?

A humorous read likely to make you a lot more sympathetic to the costuming department, "The Time-Traveller's Seamstress" is an entertaining book that will keep readers engaged to the end.

Book One of Supporting the Time-Space Continuum

Available in Paperback and Kindle ebook

The Time Traveller's Accountant

The Costuming Department probably had it worse, but life wasn't all roses in Finance, either.

Whether it was sourcing ancient coins in a usable condition, only for the Agents to lose then less than a week later, or trying to convince Management to approve a payroll system from the current century (seriously, did anyone still use paycheques for wages?), it was one problem after another.

You'd think that the other departments would be more sympathetic, given what the agents subjected them to, but no...

An entertaining sequel to the Time Traveller's Seamstress, this book is a fast-paced read that will keep you going until the end.

Book Tw0 of Supporting the Time-Space Continuum

Available in Paperback and Kindle ebook

Captive Hearts

No one was entirely sure what had started the conflict with the Grey Mountains, only that there was no end in sight.

When Danae, one of the Vale's most powerful Healers, is taken prisoner in a raid, she finds an unexpected protector: Torrin, the Mountain King's nephew. In fear for her life, Danae is determined to hate the man responsible for her capture, but his kindness and compassion make it increasingly difficult.

Torrin hadn't expected to find himself in charge of a prisoner, especially such a difficult one. He hadn't expected to find her defiance so attractive either. If only she wasn't his prisoner...

In a tale of intrigue, rivalry and love, duty and reason war with uncertain hearts to form a gripping romance.

Available in Paperback and Kindle ebook

The Murder Mystery

Ramona Bates thought that a dating site that matched people based on their internet search history was the perfect way to get everyone off her back about her lack of a love-life. Ramona was a crime fiction writer, who was going to have a google history to match that?

When she met Joshua Ryan, a butcher's assistant who knew a surprising amount about murder, it seemed like destiny.

When Ramona released her first book, the local police force realised that a lot of the murder scenes matched with old crime reports. Now they are on the hunt, but will they catch the right person?

In a twisting tale that puts a new spin on both crime and romance, this book will have you holding your breath to the end.

Available in Kindle Ebook and Paperback

Surviving a Zombie Apocalypse

No-one ever thought that the Zombie Apocalyse would actually happen.

If the average person thought about a potential Zombie Invasion at all, it was to mock unrealistic movies or discuss how/if they would survive it. That turned out to be a good thing.

When the emergency call went out that the pandemic that turned its victims into something very like Zombies was not, in fact, a viral hoax, but the real thing, they had a plan.

As it turned out, the biggest danger wasn't the Zombies, but surviving the morons who though they were living a video game and had just figured out that Loot Drops didn't exist in real life…

Available in Kindle Ebook and Paperback

The Protector

All children know about the monsters. The ones under the bed, in the closet, hiding beneath the stairs... All just waiting to jump out and attack.

Children do not know of their protectors, the ones who fight the monsters, who keep the children safe, until they are no longer needed. Sometimes, that lasts a lot longer than physical childhood.

In a tale that combines that fantasy and nostalgia of childhood with the more mature outlook of adult life, The Protector is a book that will leave you longing for more.

Available now in Kindle Ebook and Paperback